La casa de galletitas

The Cookie House

Querido padre o tutor: Es posible que los libros de esta serie para lectores principiantes les resulten familiares, ya que las versiones originales de los mismos podrían haber formado parte de sus primeras lecturas. Estos textos, cuidadosamente escritos, incluyen palabras de uso frecuente que le proveen al niño la oportunidad de familiarizarse con las más comúnmente usadas en el lenguaje escrito. Estas nuevas versiones han sido actualizadas y las encantadoras ilustraciones son sumamente atractivas para una nueva generación de pequeños lectores.

Primero, léale el cuento al niño, después permita que él lea las palabras con las que esté familiarizado, y pronto podrá leer solito todo el cuento. En cada paso, elogie el esfuerzo del niño para que desarrolle confianza como lector independiente. Hable sobre las ilustraciones y anime al niño a relacionar el cuento con su propia vida.

Al final del cuento, encontrará actividades relacionadas con la lectura que ayudarán a su niño a practicar y fortalecer sus habilidades como lector. Estas actividades, junto con las preguntas de comprensión, se adhieren a los estándares actuales, de manera que la lectura en casa apoyará directamente los objetivos de instrucción en el salón de clase.

Sobre todo, la parte más importante de toda la experiencia de la lectura es ¡divertirse y disfrutarla!

Dear Caregiver: The books in this Beginning-to-Read collection may look somewhat familiar in that the original versions could have been a part of your own early reading experiences. These carefully written texts feature common sight words to provide your child multiple exposures to the words appearing most frequently in written text. These new versions have been updated and the engaging illustrations are highly appealing to a contemporary audience of young readers.

Begin by reading the story to your child, followed by letting him or her read familiar words and soon your child will be able to read the story independently. At each step of the way, be sure to praise your reader's efforts to build his or her confidence as an independent reader. Discuss the pictures and encourage your child to make connections between the story and his or her own life.

At the end of the story, you will find reading activities that will help your child practice and strengthen beginning reading skills. These activities, along with the comprehension questions are aligned to current standards, so reading efforts at home will directly support the instructional goals in the classroom.

Above all, the most important part of the reading experience is to have fun and enjoy it!

Shannon Cannon

Shannon Cannon, Ph.D., Consultora de lectoescritura / Literacy Consultant

Norwood House Press • www.norwoodhousepress.com
Beginning-to-Read ™ is a registered trademark of Norwood House Press.
Illustration and cover design copyright ©2018 by Norwood House Press. All Rights Reserved.

Authorized Bilingual adaptation from the U.S. English language edition, entitled The Cookie House by Margaret Hillert. Copyright © 2017 Margaret Hillert. Bilingual adaptation Copyright © 2018 Margaret Hillert. Translated and adapted with permission. All rights reserved. Pearson and La casa de galletitas are trademarks, in the US and/or other countries, of Pearson Education, Inc. or its affiliates. This publication is protected by copyright, and prior permission to re-use in any way in any format is required by both Norwood House Press and Pearson Education. This book is authorized in the United States for use in schools and public libraries.

Designer: Ron Jaffe • Editorial Production: Lisa Walsh

LIBRARY OF CONGRESS CATALOGING-IN-PUBLICATION DATA

Names: Hillert, Margaret, author. | Utomo, Gabhor, illustrator. | Del Risco, Eida, translator.
Title: La casa de galletitas = The cookie house / por Margaret Hillert ; ilustrado por Gabhor Utomo ; traducido por Eida Del Risco.
Other titles: Cookie house | Hansel and Gretel. English.
Description: Chicago, Illinois : Norwood House Press, [2017] | Series: A beginning-to-read book | Summary: "An easy to read fairy tale about Hansel and Gretel and their trip through the forest. Spanish/English edition includes reading activities"-- Provided by publisher.
Identifiers: LCCN 2016057979 (print) | LCCN 2017014221 (ebook) | ISBN 9781684040568 (eBook) | ISBN 9781599538426 (library edition : alk. paper)
Subjects: | CYAC: Fairy tales. | Folklore--Germany. | Spanish language materials--Bilingual.
Classification: LCC PZ74 (ebook) | LCC PZ74 .H4434 2017 (print) | DDC 398.2 [E] --dc23
LC record available at https://lccn.loc.gov/2016057979

Hardcover ISBN: 978-1-59953-842-6   Paperback ISBN: 978-1-68404-041-4

302N—072017
Manufactured in the United States of America in North Mankato, Minnesota.

La casa de galletitas

The Cookie House

Hansel y Gretel/Hansel and Gretel
Contado por/Retold by Margaret Hillert
Ilustrado por/Illustrated by Gabhor Utomo

NORWOOD HOUSE  PRESS

Levántense, levántense.
Vengan con nosotros.
Vamos a ir a trabajar.

Get up. Get up.
Come with us.
We will go to work.

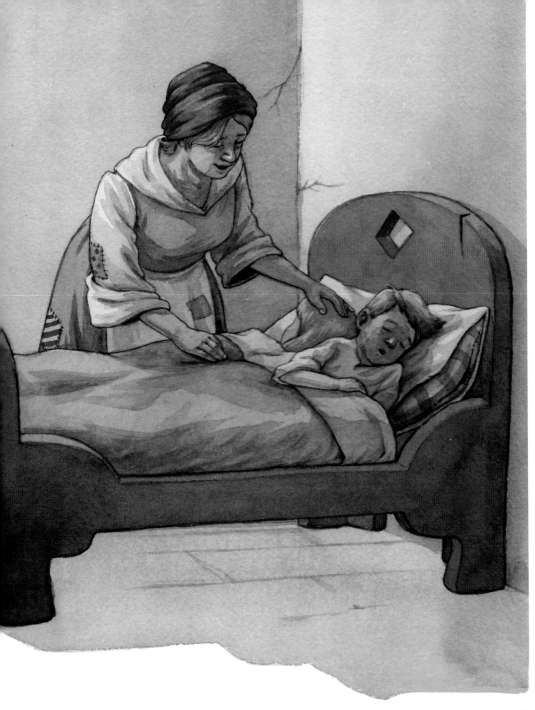

Ay, esto es divertido.
Podemos correr y saltar.
Nos gusta aquí.

Oh, this is fun.
We can run and jump.
We like it here.

Jueguen aquí.
No tienen que trabajar.
Ahora nosotros nos vamos.
Pero vamos a volver
a buscarlos.

You two play here.
You do not have to work.
We will go now.
But we will come back
to get you.

9

Mira.
Aquí hay algo para nosotros.
Algo que nos gusta.
Toma una.

Look here.
Here is something for us.
Something we like.
Have one.

Y aquí hay algo.
Es pequeña.
Puede jugar con nosotros.

And here is something.
It is little.
It can play with us.

Mamá no está aquí.
Papá no está aquí.
No me gusta esto.

Mother is not here.
Father is not here.
I do not like this.

No podemos encontrar el camino.
¿Qué podemos hacer ahora?
¿Quién nos ayudará?
Quiero volver.

We can not find the way.
What can we do now?
Who will help us?
I want to go.

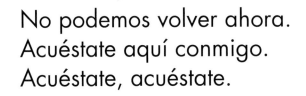

No podemos volver ahora.
Acuéstate aquí conmigo.
Acuéstate, acuéstate.

We can not go now.
Come down here with me.
Come down, down, down.

Levántate. Levántate.   Get up. Get up.
Mira lo que veo.   Look what I see.
¿Lo ves tú también?   Can you see it, too?
Mira arriba, arriba.   Look up, up.

Míralo como se va.
También podemos ir.
Corre, corre, corre.

Look at it go.
We can go, too.
Run, run, run.

Ay, mira la casita.
Me gusta.
Me gusta.
Será divertido para nosotros.

Oh, see the little house.
I like it.
I like it.
What fun for us.

17

Mira esto y esto y esto.
Yo quiero una.
Tú también puedes comer una.

Look at this and this and this.
I want one.
You can have one, too.

19

No, no pueden.
No pueden comerse eso.
No es para ustedes.

No, you can not.
You can not have that.
It is not for you.

Ay, ayuda, ayuda.
No me gusta estar aquí dentro.
Ayúdame, ayúdame.

Oh, help, help.
I do not like it in here.
Help me. Help me.

Aquí estoy.
Te voy a ayudar.
Mira como te ayudo.

Here I come.
I will help you.
See me help.

Entra. Entra.
No te queremos.
Haré que entres.
Vas para adentro.

Go in. Go in.
We do not like you.
I will make you go in.
In you go.

23

Nos vamos.
Nos vamos.

Come away.
Come away.

Por aquí vamos.
Corre, corre, corre.

Here we go.
Run, run, run.

¿Qué es esto?
¿Qué podemos hacer ahora?
No podemos seguir.

What is this?
What can we do now?
We can not go in here.

Ay, mira dónde estamos.
Qué divertido.
¡Esto sí es un paseo!

Oh, look at us.
What fun.
What a ride this is!

Veo a papá.
Papá, papá.
Aquí estamos, papá.

I see Father.
Father, Father.
Here we are, Father.

Foundational Skills

In addition to reading the numerous high-frequency words in the text, this book also supports the development of foundational skills.

Phonological Awareness: The /k/ sound

Oddity Task: Say the **/k/** sound for your child. Ask your child to say the word that has the **/k/** sound in the following word groups:

kid, rid, bid	rot, run, rock	pan, pat, pack
dot, Don, dock	Sam, sat, sack	rind, kind, mind

Phonics: The letter Kk

1. Demonstrate how to form the letters **k** and **k** for your child.
2. Have your child practice writing **k** and **k** at least three times each.
3. Write down the following words and ask your child to circle the letter **k** in each word:

back	kit	make	king	rocket
look	work	like	lock	kitten
bucket	truck	key	milk	chicken

Fluency: Echo Reading

1. Reread the story to your child at least two more times while your child tracks the print by running a finger under the words as they are read. Ask your child to read the words he or she knows with you.
2. Reread the story, stopping after each sentence or page to allow your child to read (echo) what you have read. Repeat echo reading and let your child take the lead.

Language

The concepts, illustrations, and text help children develop language both explicitly and implicitly.

Vocabulary: Nouns and Verbs

1. Write the following words on separate pieces of paper and point to them as you read them to your child:

go	mother	house	jump	father
boy	work	run	girl	tree

2. Point to each word and read it aloud to your child. Ask your child to repeat the word.
3. Explain to your child that words describing people, places, and things are called nouns and that words describing actions are called verbs.
4. Divide a piece of paper in half vertically and write the words nouns and verbs at the top, one word in each column.
5. Ask your child to sort the words on the pieces of paper by placing them in the correct column depending on whether the word on the paper is a noun or a verb.
6. Continue identifying nouns and verbs by playing a game in which one of you names a noun and the other names a verb to go with the noun (for example; dog/bark, baby/cry, grass/grow, flower/bloom, car/drive, etc.)

Reading Literature and Informational Text

To support comprehension, ask your child the following questions. The answers either come directly from the text or require inferences and discussion.

Key Ideas and Detail

- Ask your child to retell the sequence of events in the story.
- What happened when the children ate the treats off of the house?

Craft and Structure

- Is this a book that tells a story or one that gives information? How do you know?
- How do you think the boy and girl felt when they got lost?

Integration of Knowledge and Ideas

- Would you have eaten the cookies on the house? Why or why not?
- What lessons do you think the children learned?

Margaret Hillert ha ayudado a millones de niños de todo el mundo a aprender a leer independientemente. Fue maestra de primer grado por 34 años y durante esa época empezó a escribir libros con los que sus estudiantes pudieran ganar confianza en la lectura y pudieran, al mismo tiempo, disfrutarla. Ha escrito más de 100 libros para niños que comienzan a leer. De niña, disfrutaba escribiendo poesía y, de adulta, continuó su escritura poética tanto para niños como para adultos.

Photograph by Glenna Washburn

Margaret Hillert has helped millions of children all over the world learn to read independently. She was a first grade teacher for 34 years and during that time started writing books that her students could both gain confidence in reading and enjoy. She wrote well over 100 books for children just learning to read. As a child, she enjoyed writing poetry and continued her poetic writings as an adult for both children and adults.

Gabhor Utomo es un artista e ilustrador independiente. Su obra ha adornado las páginas de muchos gratos libros para niños, materiales educativos, religiosos y obras comerciales. Ha ganado muchos premios de arte nacionales y locales. Reside en el Noroeste de Estados Unidos con su esposa y sus dos hijas gemelas. www.gabhorutomo.com

Gabhor Utomo is a freelance artist and illustrator. His work has graced the pages of many enjoyable children's books, educational materials, religious curriculum and commercial works. He is the recipient of numerous local and national art awards. He resides in the Northwest with his wife and twin daughters. www.gabhorutomo.com